Dear Parents:

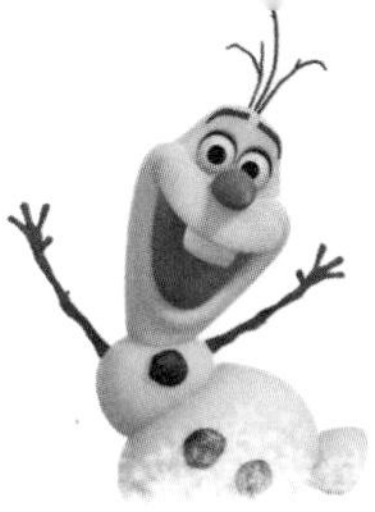

Congratulations! Your child is taking the first steps on an exciting journey. The destination? Independent reading!

STEP INTO READING® will help your child get there. The program offers five steps to reading success. Each step includes fun stories and colorful art or photographs. In addition to original fiction and books with favorite characters, there are Step into Reading Non-Fiction Readers, Phonics Readers and Boxed Sets, Sticker Readers, and Comic Readers—a complete literacy program with something to interest every child.

Learning to Read, Step by Step!

STEP 1
Ready to Read **Preschool–Kindergarten**
• big type and easy words • rhyme and rhythm • picture clues
For children who know the alphabet and are eager to begin reading.

STEP 2
Reading with Help **Preschool–Grade 1**
• basic vocabulary • short sentences • simple stories
For children who recognize familiar words and sound out new words with help.

STEP 3
Reading on Your Own **Grades 1–3**
• engaging characters • easy-to-follow plots • popular topics
For children who are ready to read on their own.

STEP 4
Reading Paragraphs **Grades 2–3**
• challenging vocabulary • short paragraphs • exciting stories
For newly independent readers who read simple sentences with confidence.

STEP 5
Ready for Chapters **Grades 2–4**
• chapters • longer paragraphs • full-color art
For children who want to take the plunge into chapter books but still like colorful pictures.

STEP INTO READING® is designed to give every child a successful reading experience. The grade levels are only guides; children will progress through the steps at their own speed, developing confidence in their reading.

Remember, a lifetime love of reading starts with a single step!

Published in the United States by Random House Children's Books, a division of Random House LLC, 1745 Broadway, New York, NY 10019, and in Canada by Random House of Canada Limited, Toronto, Penguin Random House Companies, in conjunction with Disney Enterprises, Inc.

Visit us on the Web!
StepIntoReading.com
randomhousekids.com

Educators and librarians, for a variety of teaching tools, visit us at
RHTeachersLibrarians.com

ISBN 978-0-7364-3433-1 (trade) — ISBN 978-0-7364-8240-0 (lib. bdg.)
ISBN 978-0-7364-3434-8 (ebook)

Printed in the United States of America

10 9 8 7 6 5 4 3 2 1

STEP 1 STEP INTO READING®
READY TO READ

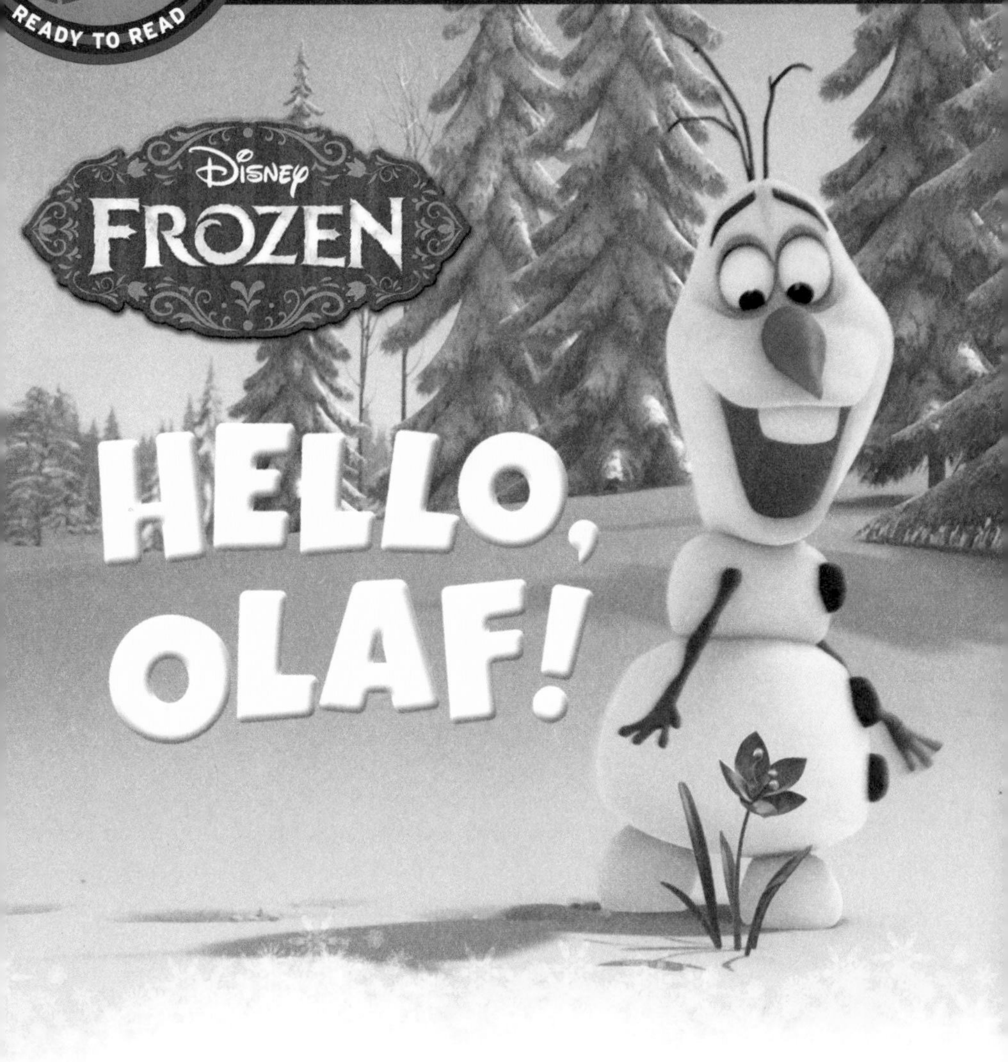

Disney FROZEN

HELLO, OLAF!

By Andrea Posner-Sanchez

Random House New York

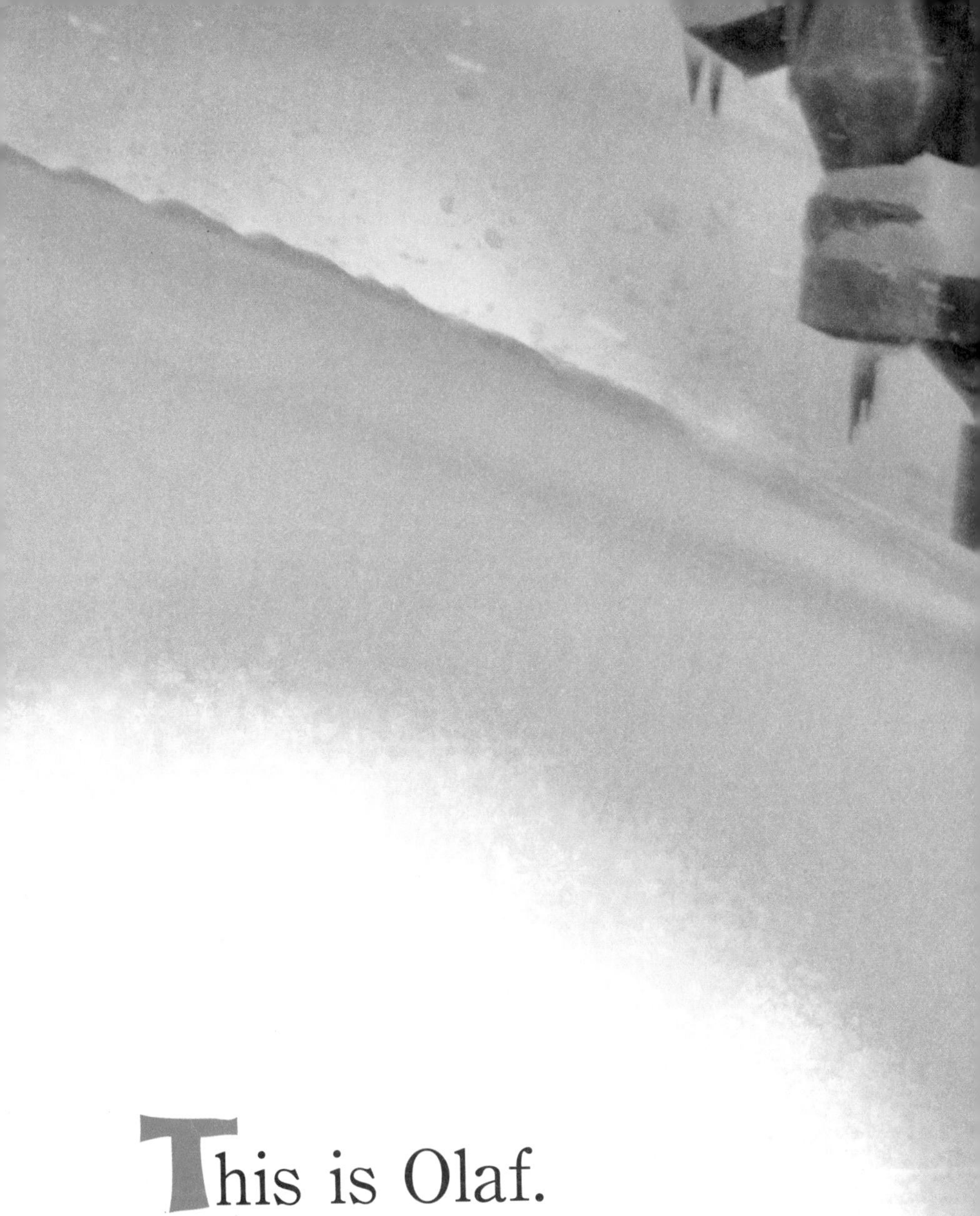

This is Olaf.

He is a snowman.

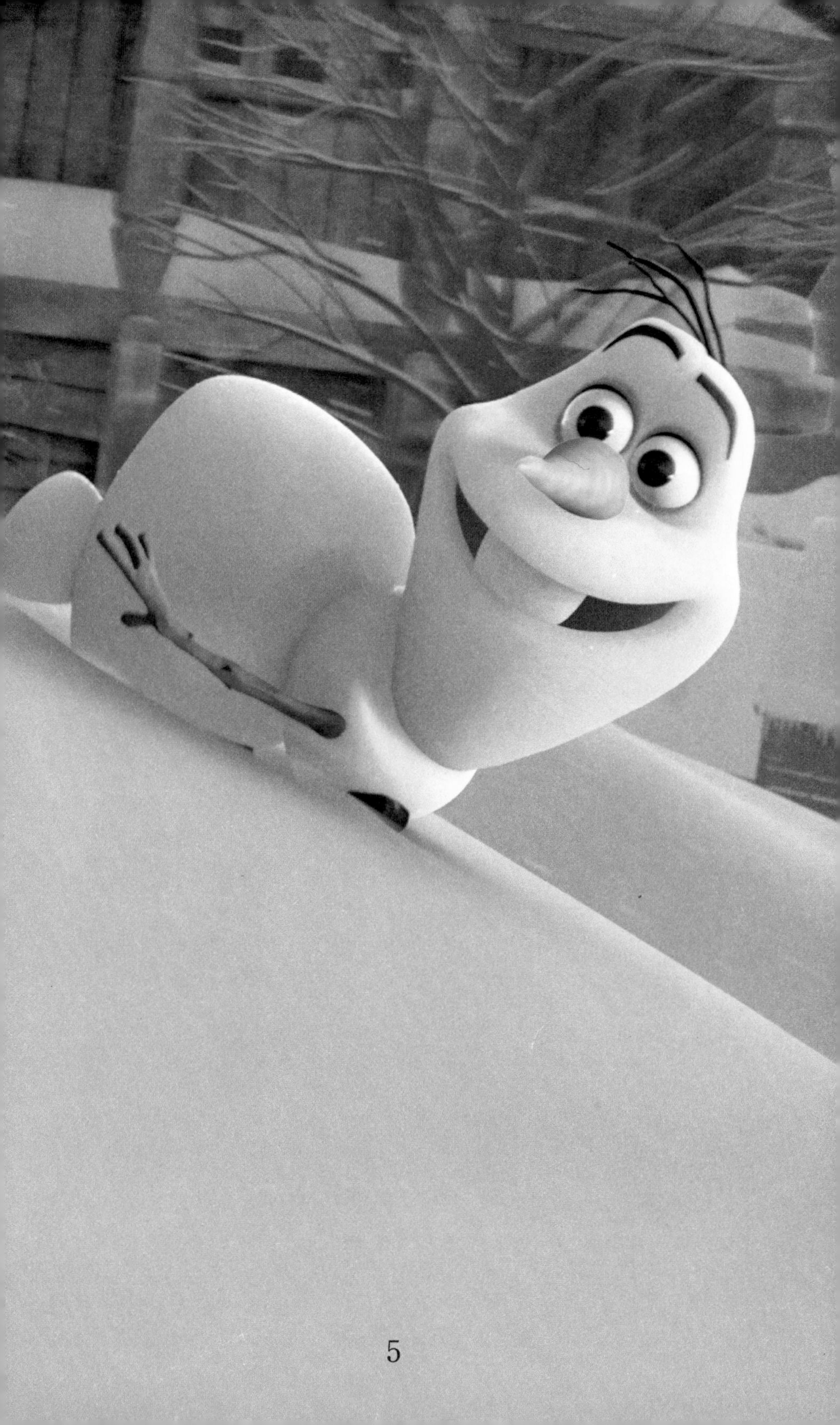

Elsa made a snowman
to play with when she
was a little girl.
Elsa and Anna called
the snowman Olaf.
They pretended he
was alive.

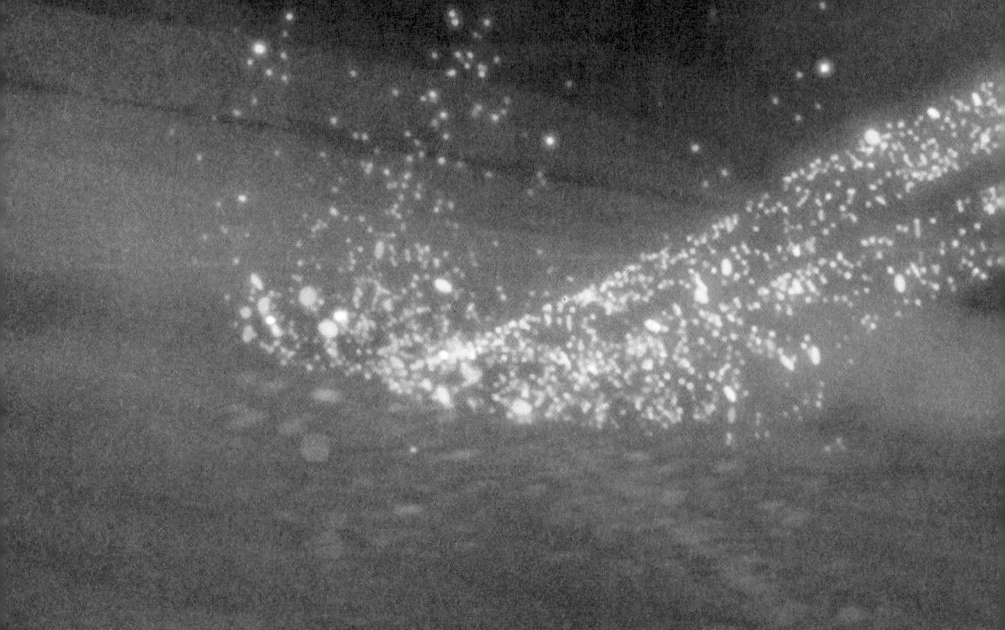

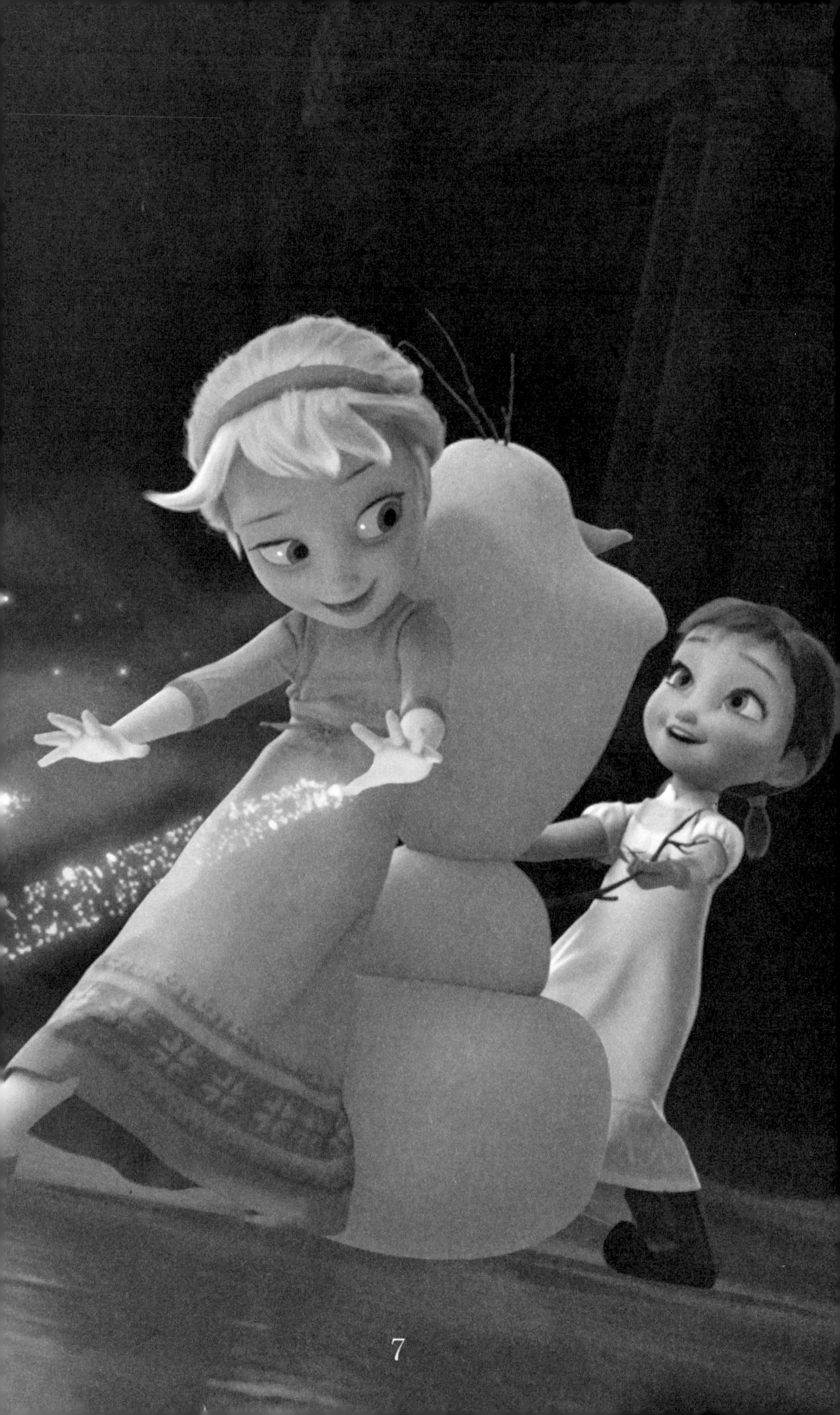

Years later, Elsa uses her magical powers to really make Olaf come to life!

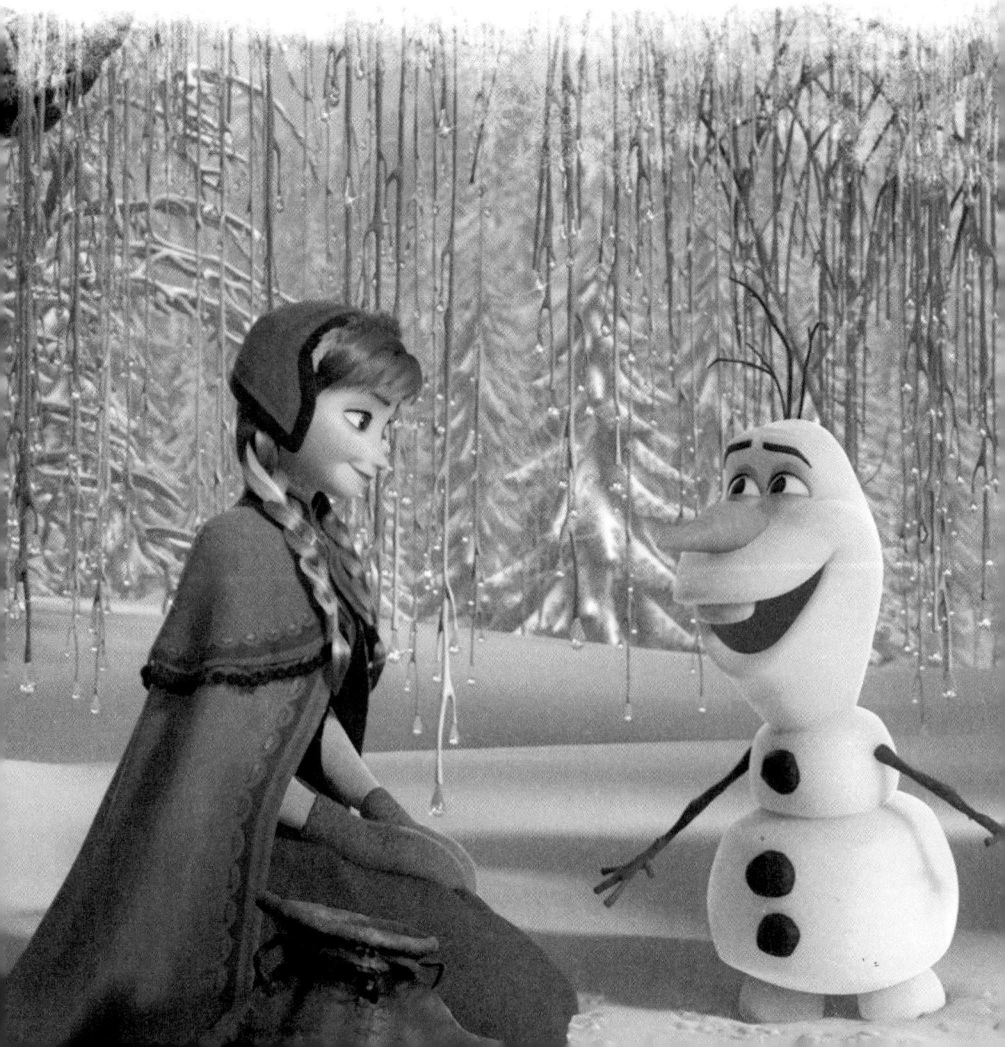

Anna is all

grown up now.

Olaf meets Anna,

Kristoff, and Sven.

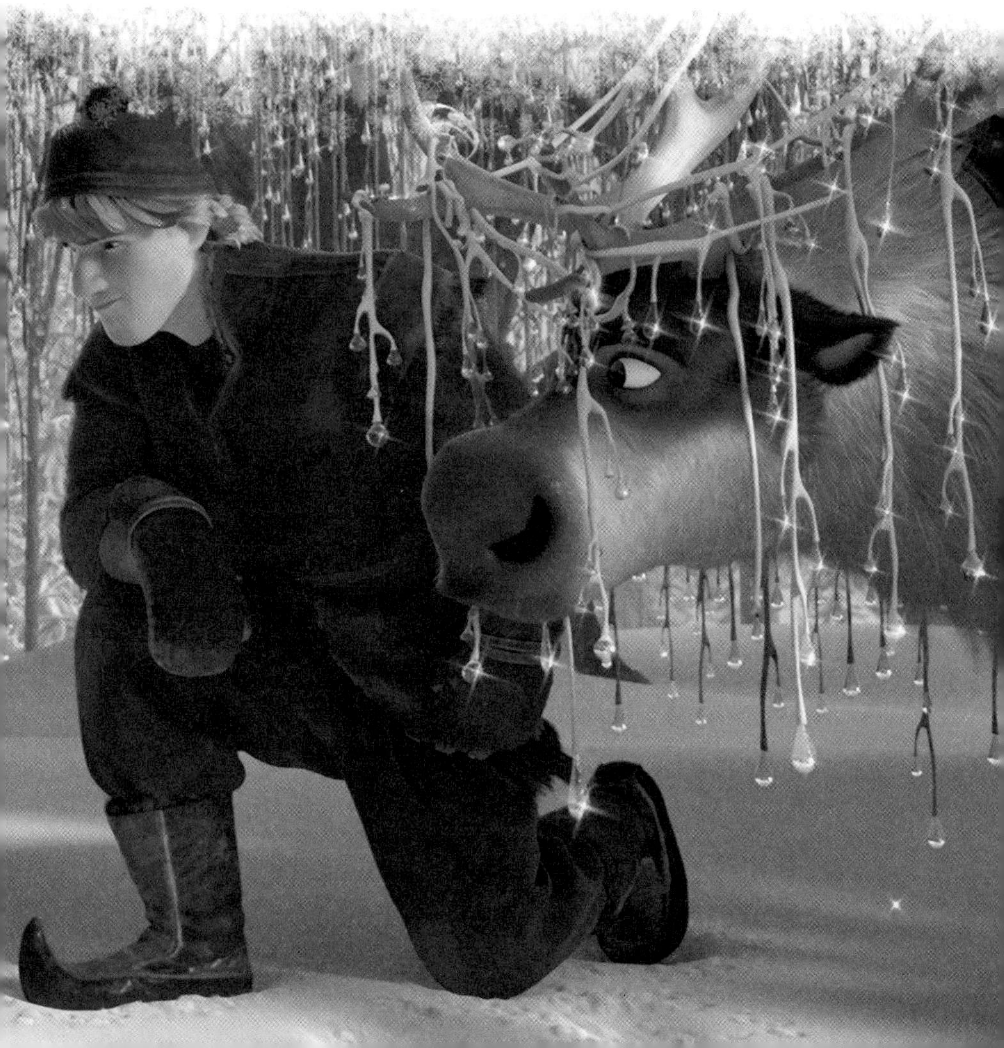

Sven loves carrots.

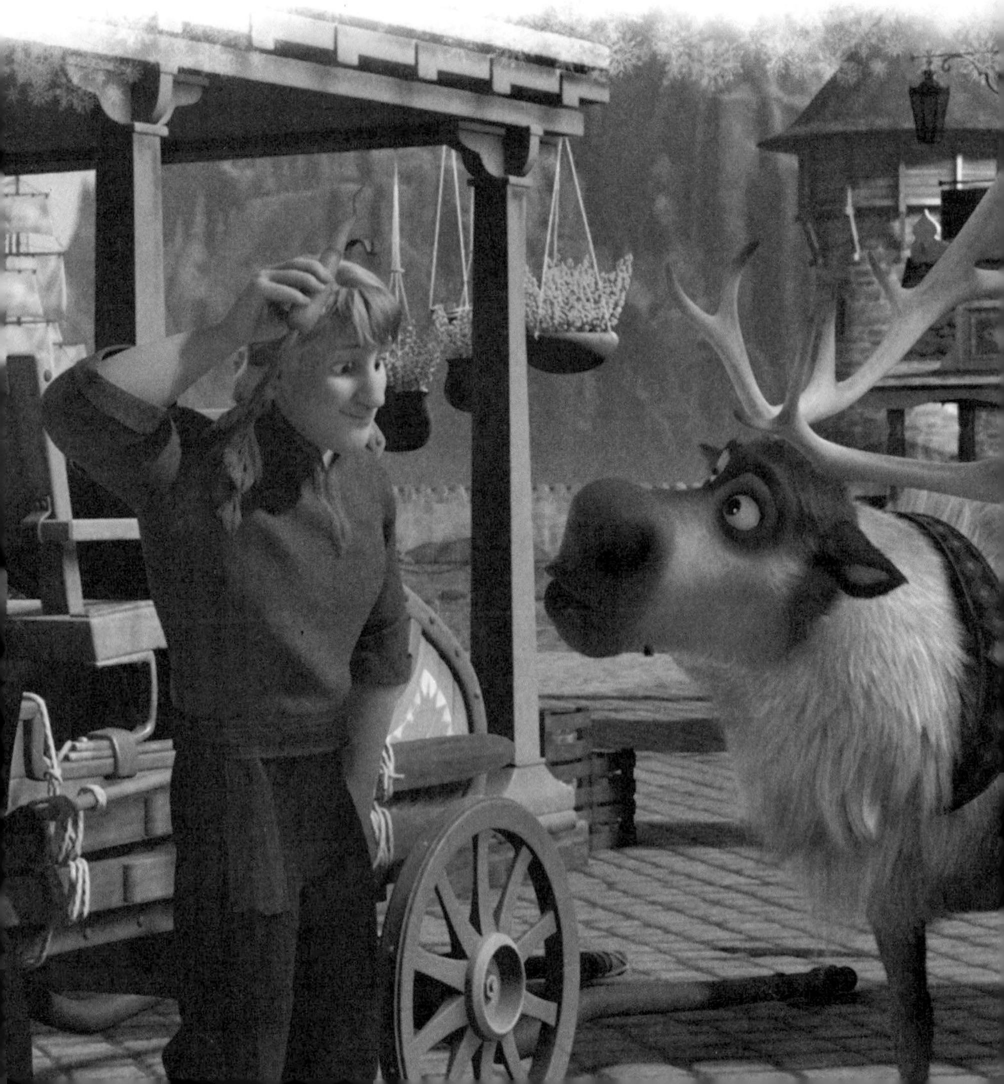

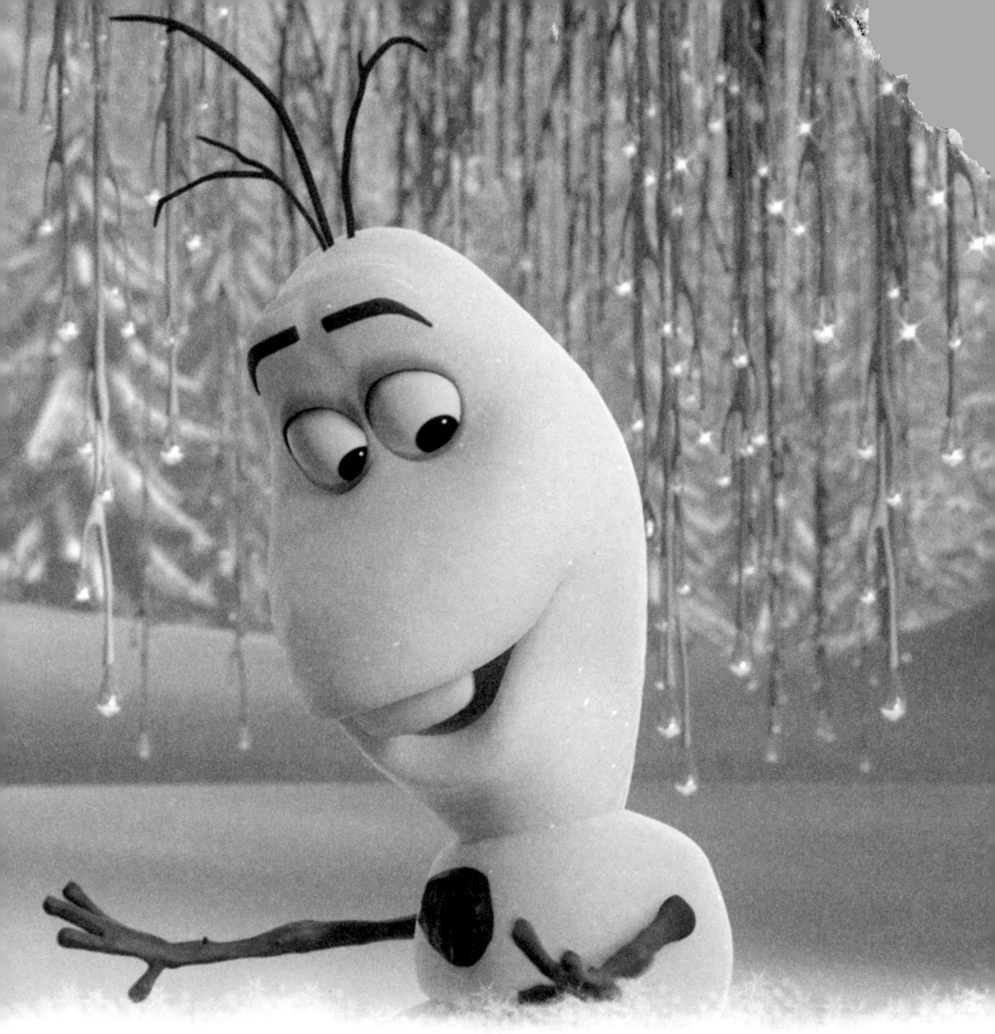

Olaf better hold on
to his nose!

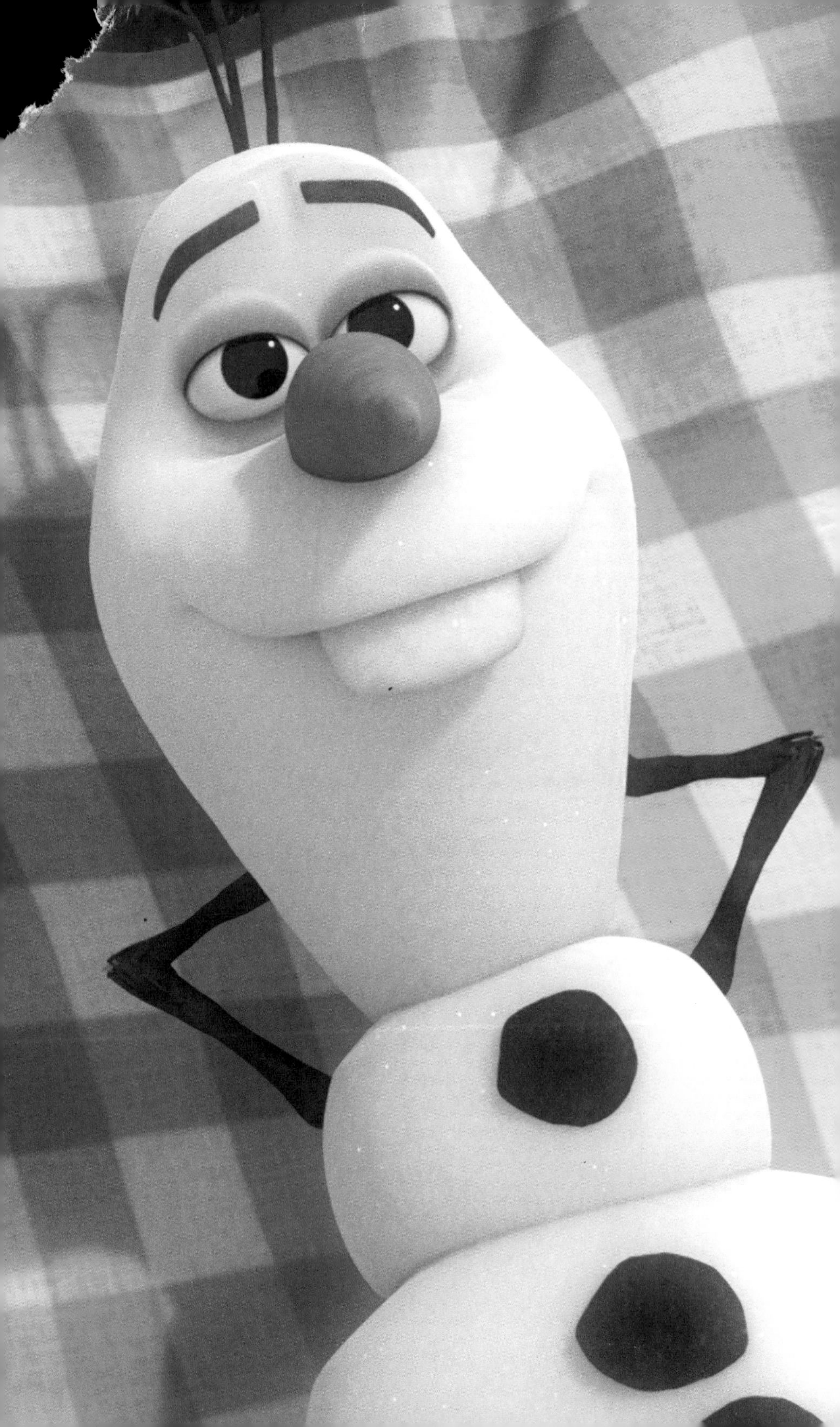

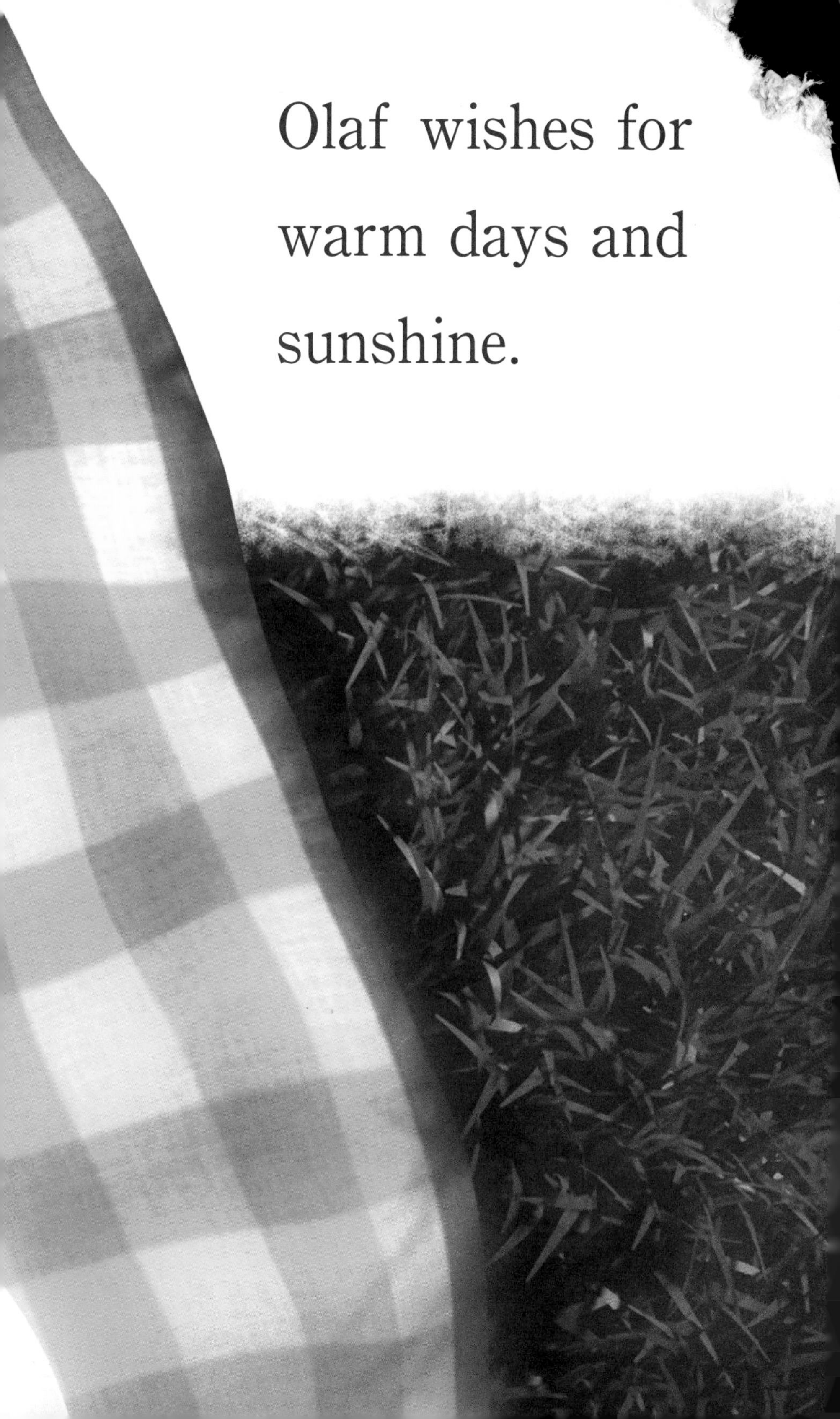

Olaf wishes for
warm days and
sunshine.

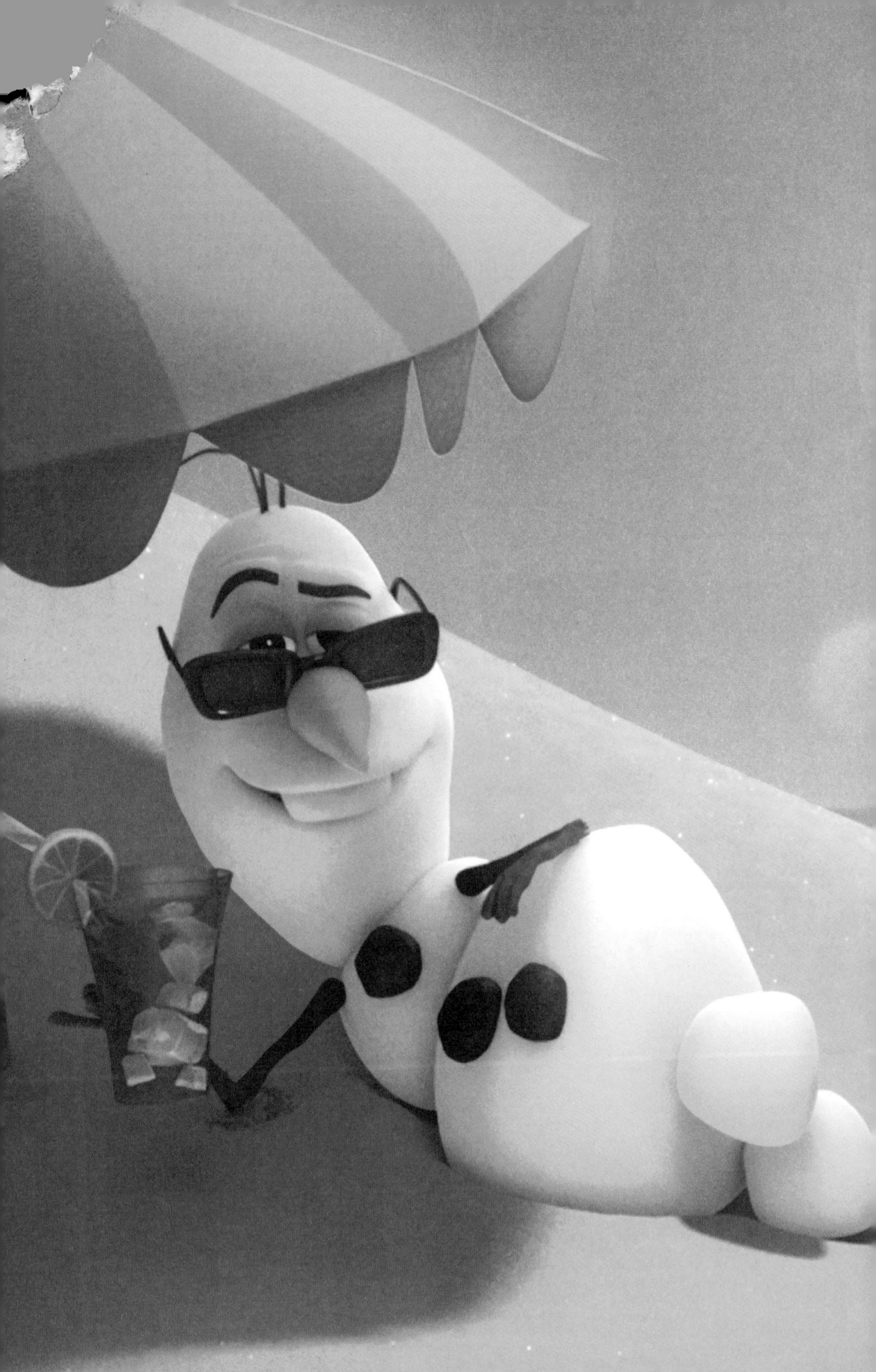

A day on the beach
would be a dream
come true!

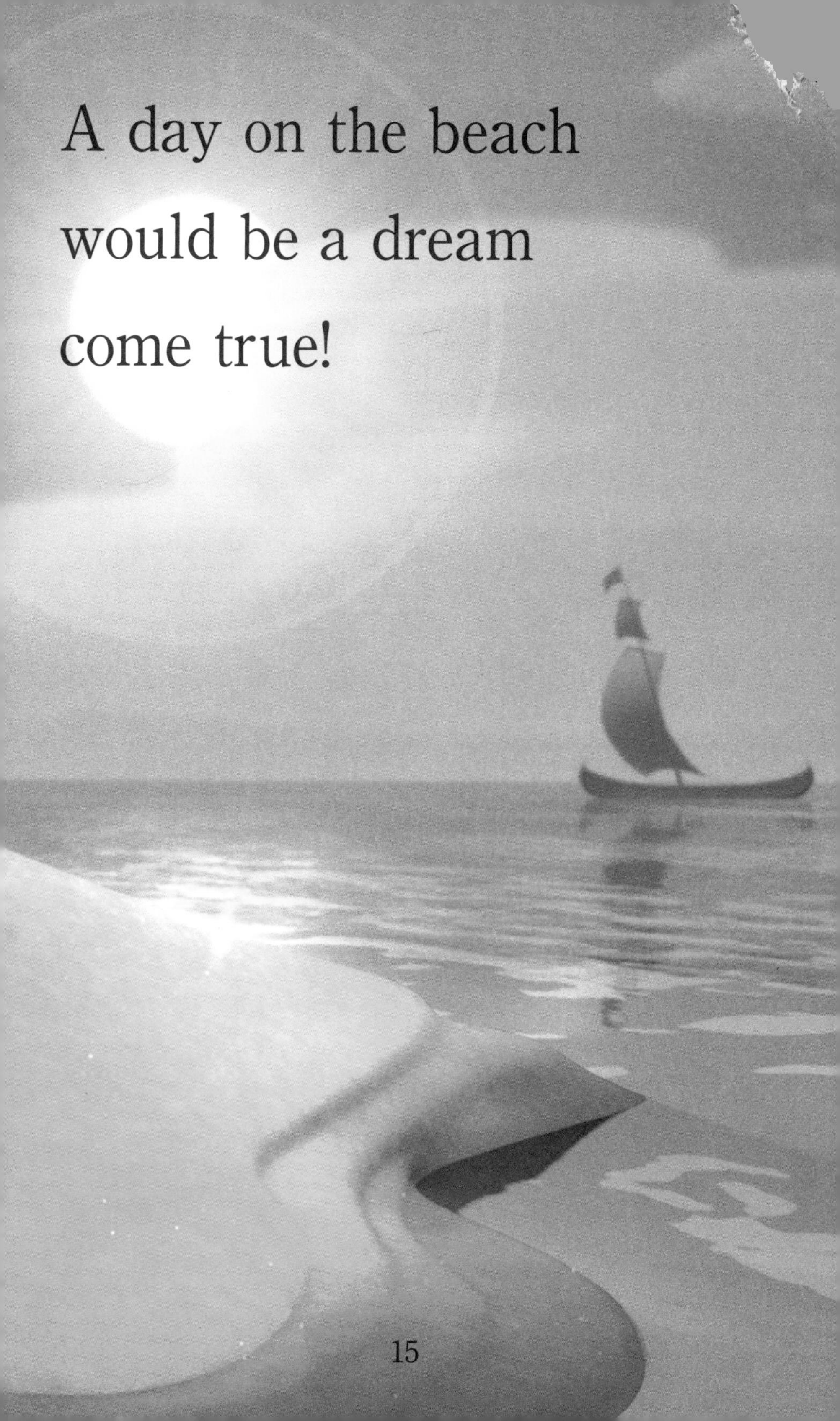

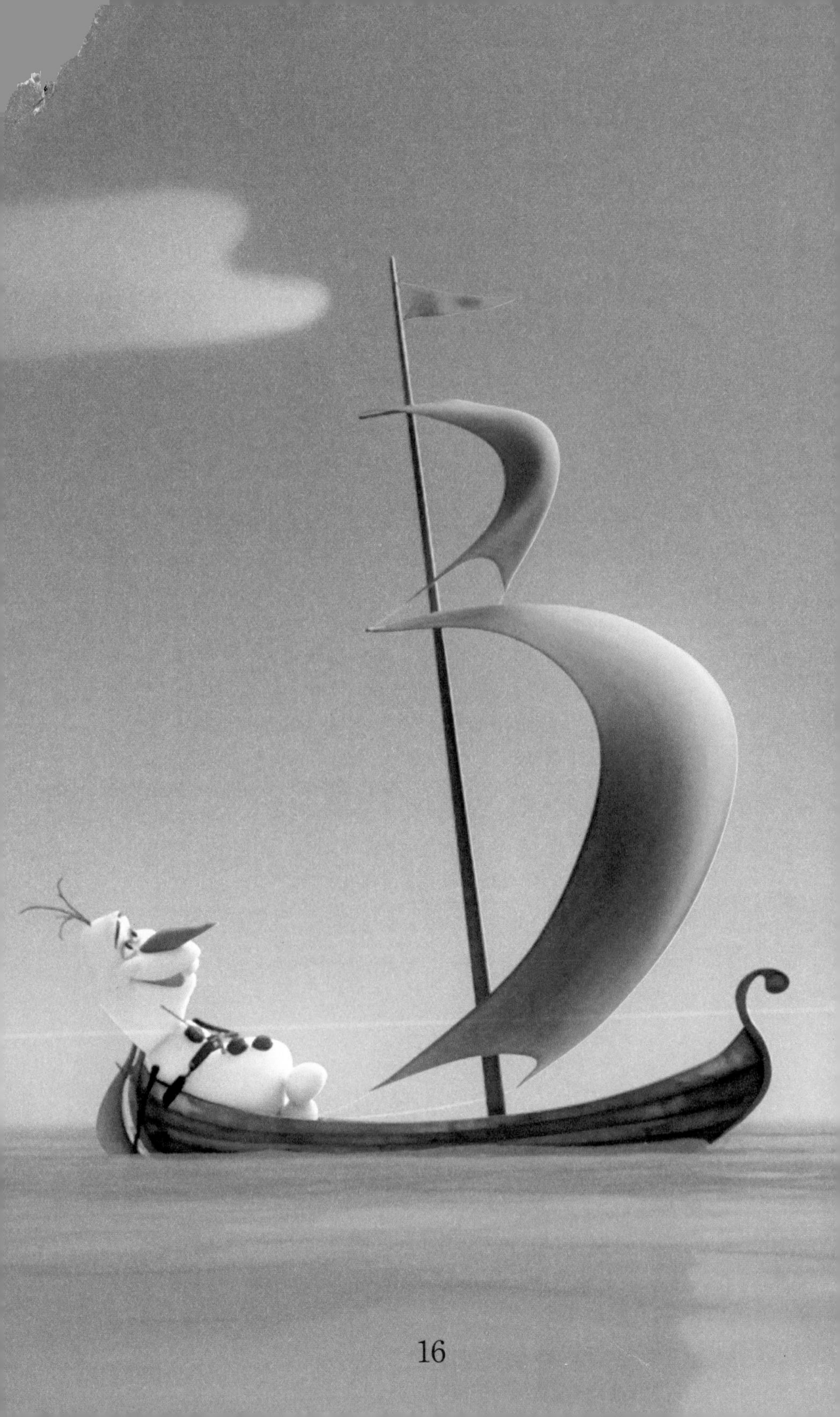

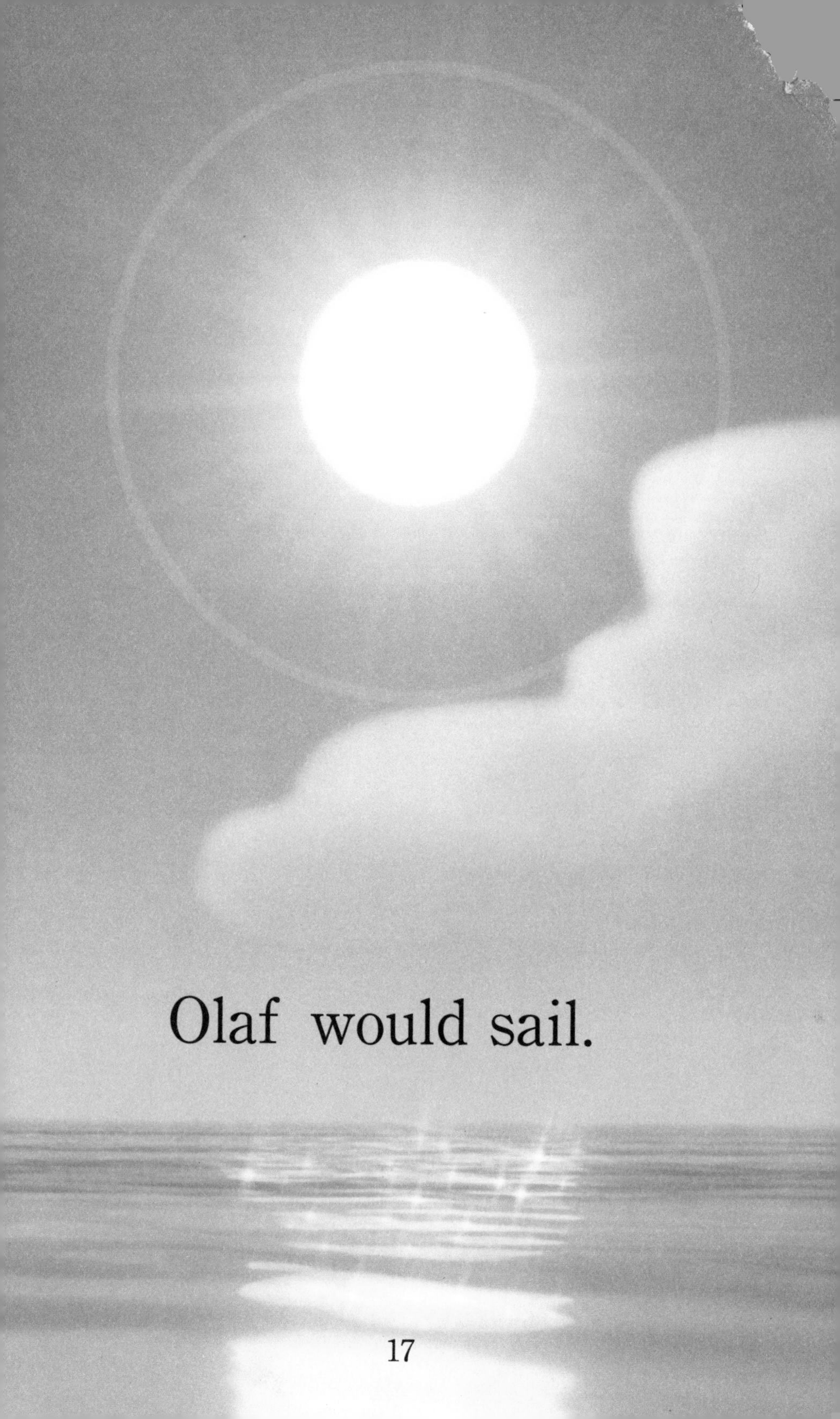

Olaf would sail.

Olaf would swim.

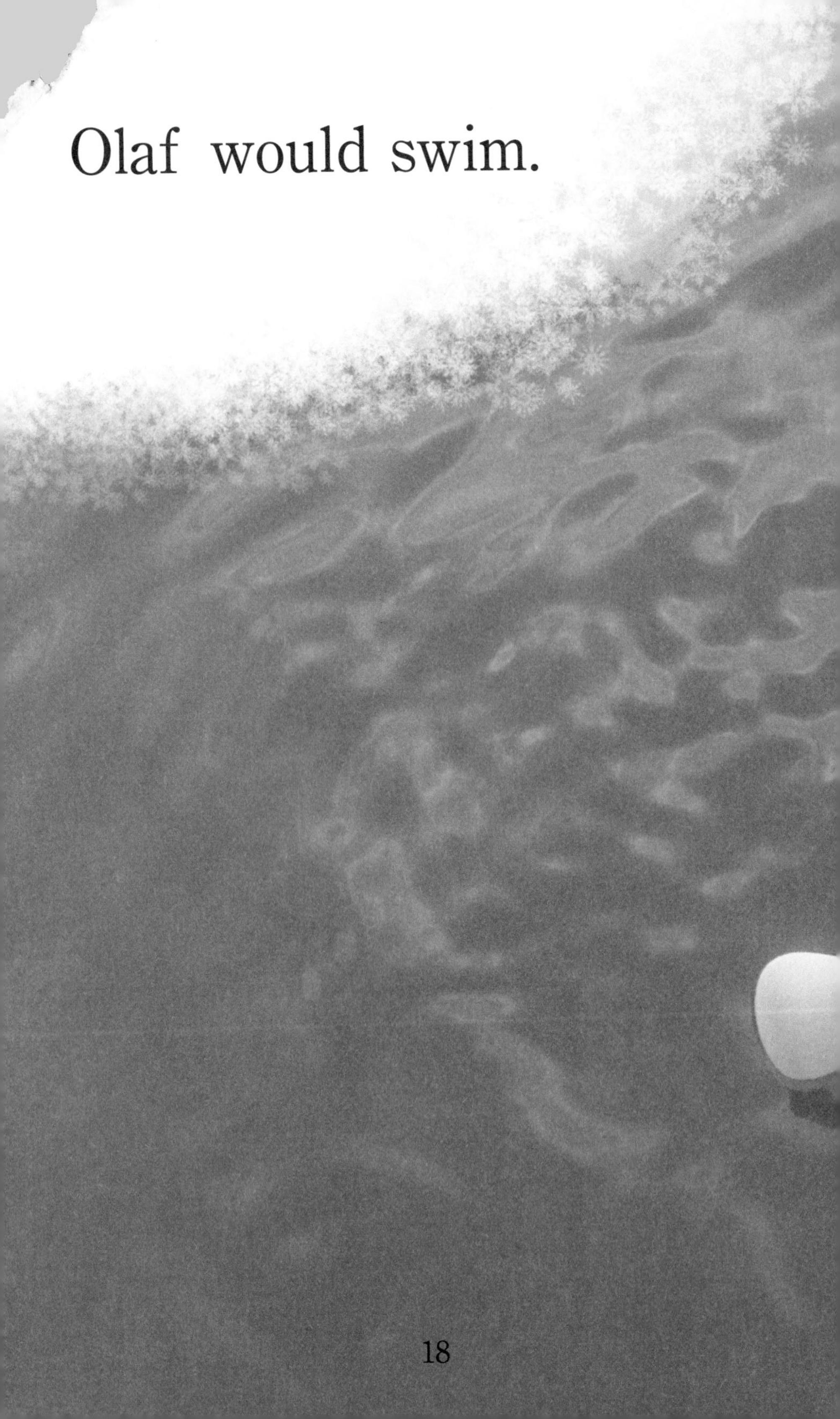

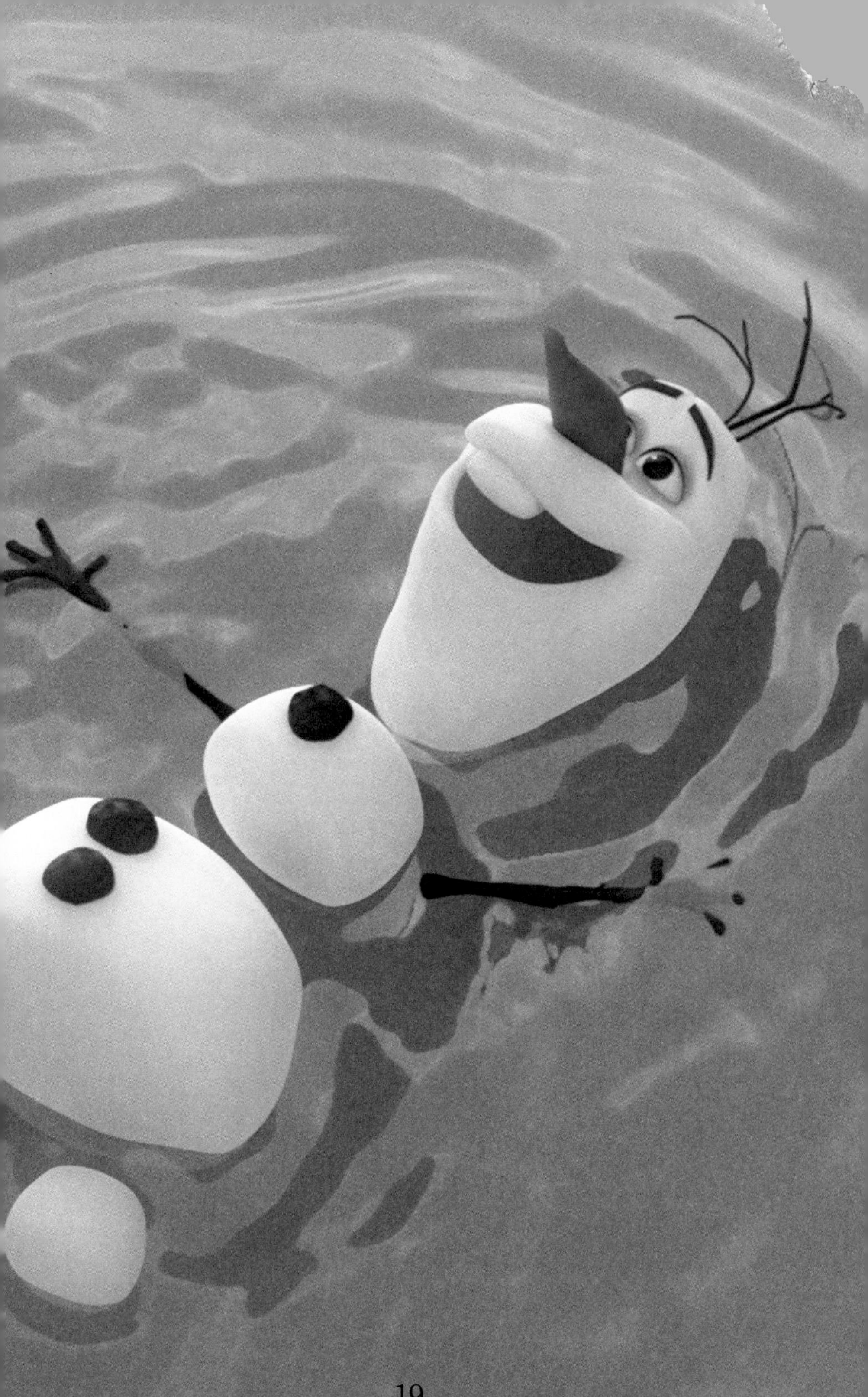

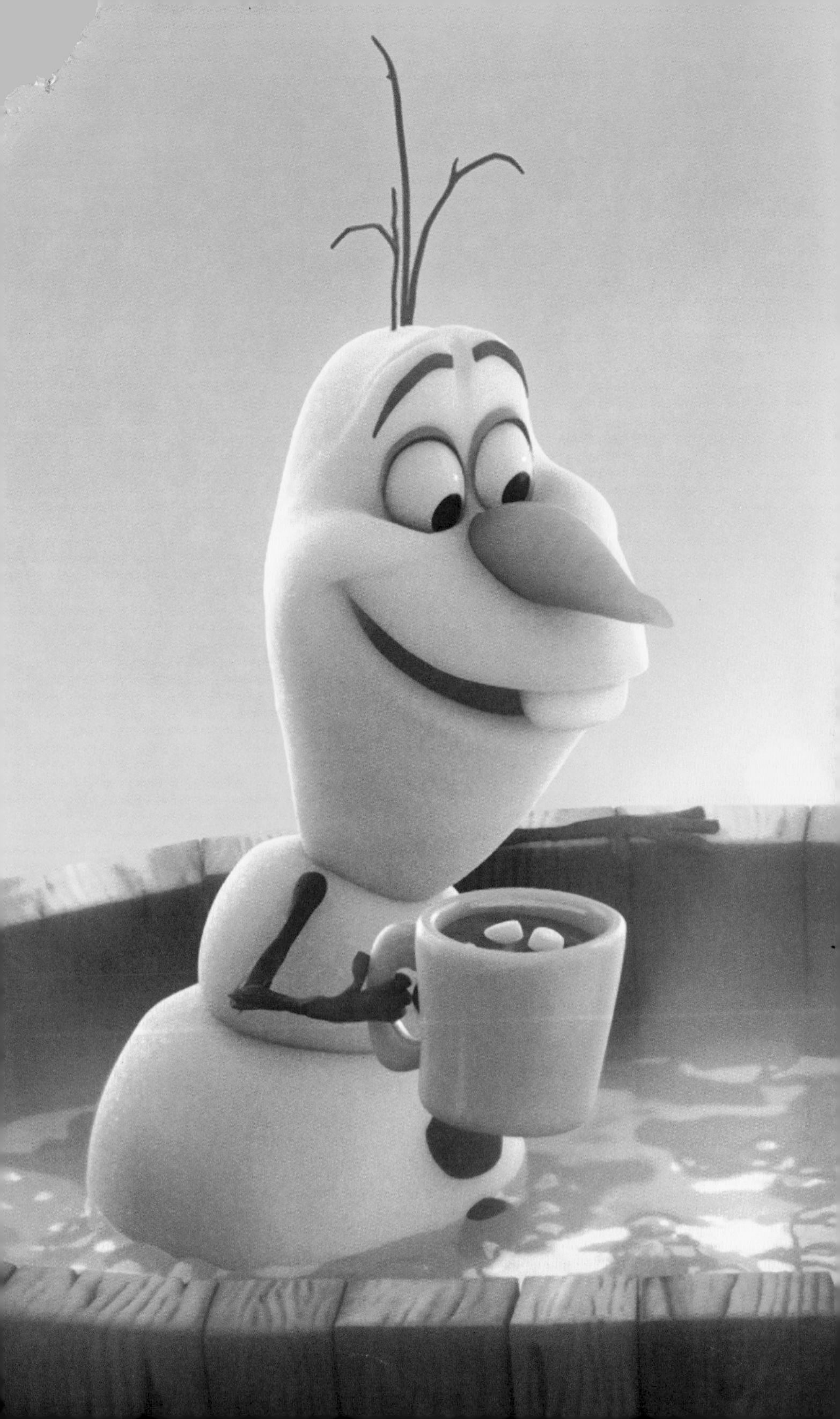

He would even sit
in a hot tub.
Do not melt, Olaf!

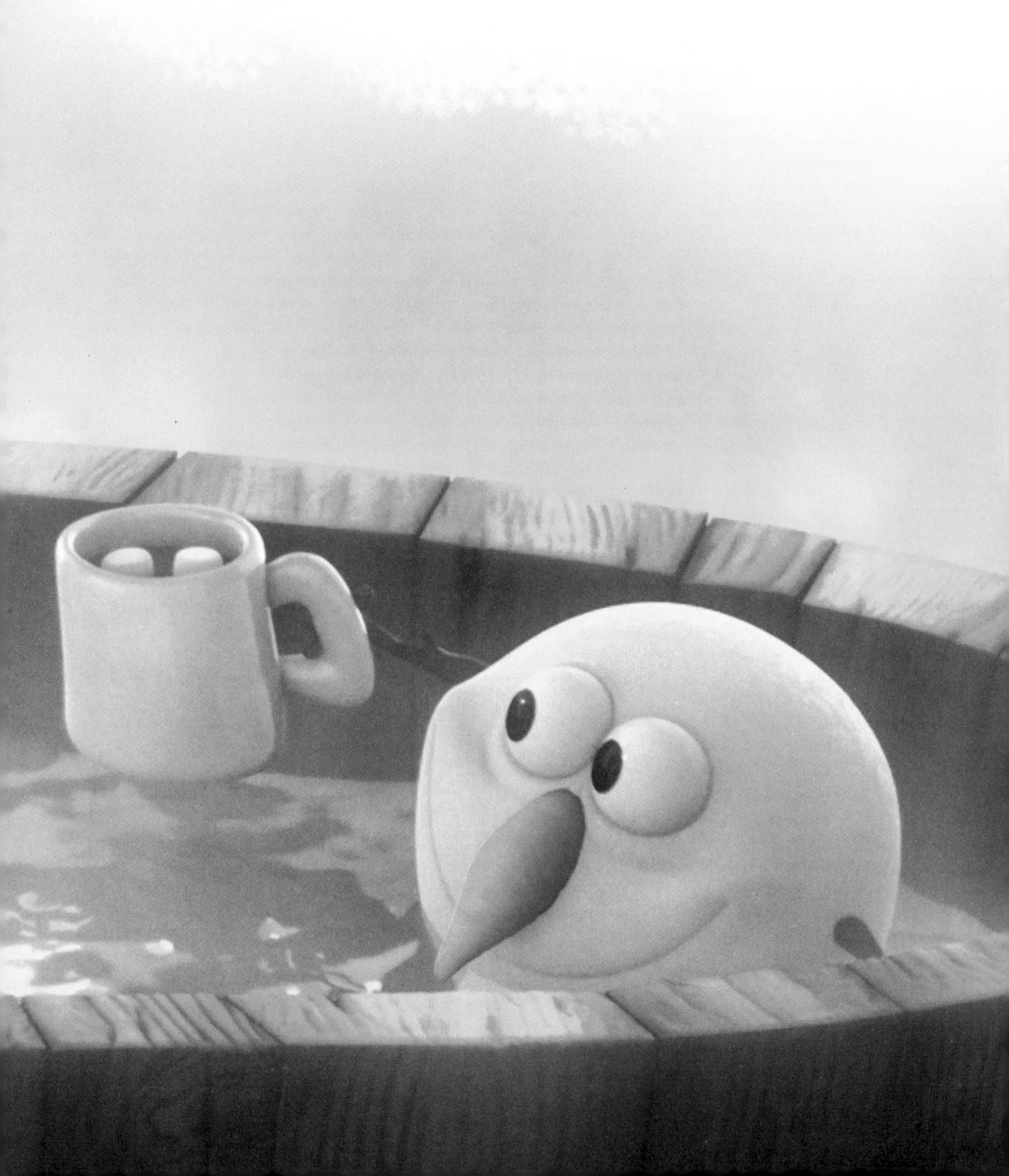

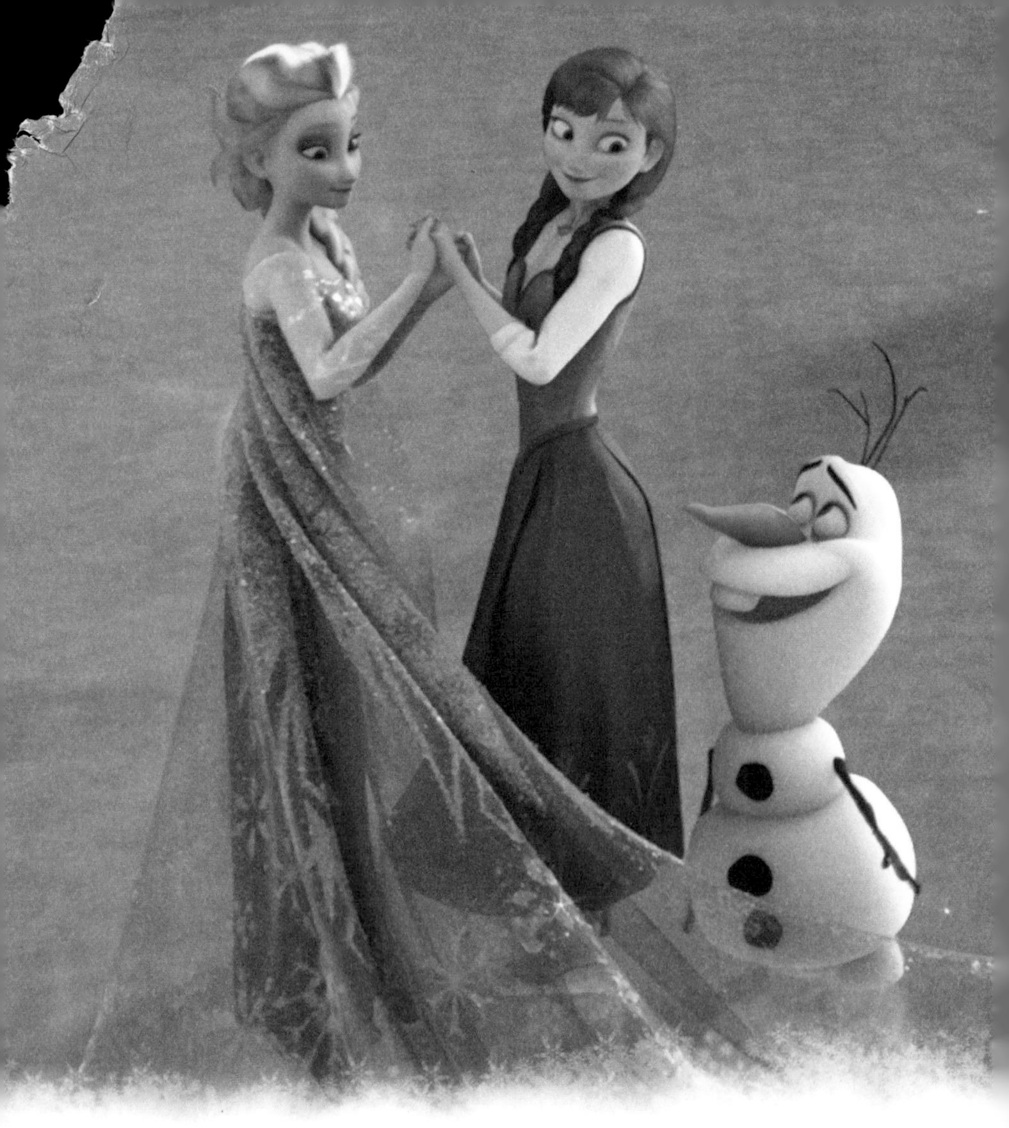

Elsa has a way
to keep Olaf cold
even when it is warm.

She does some magic.

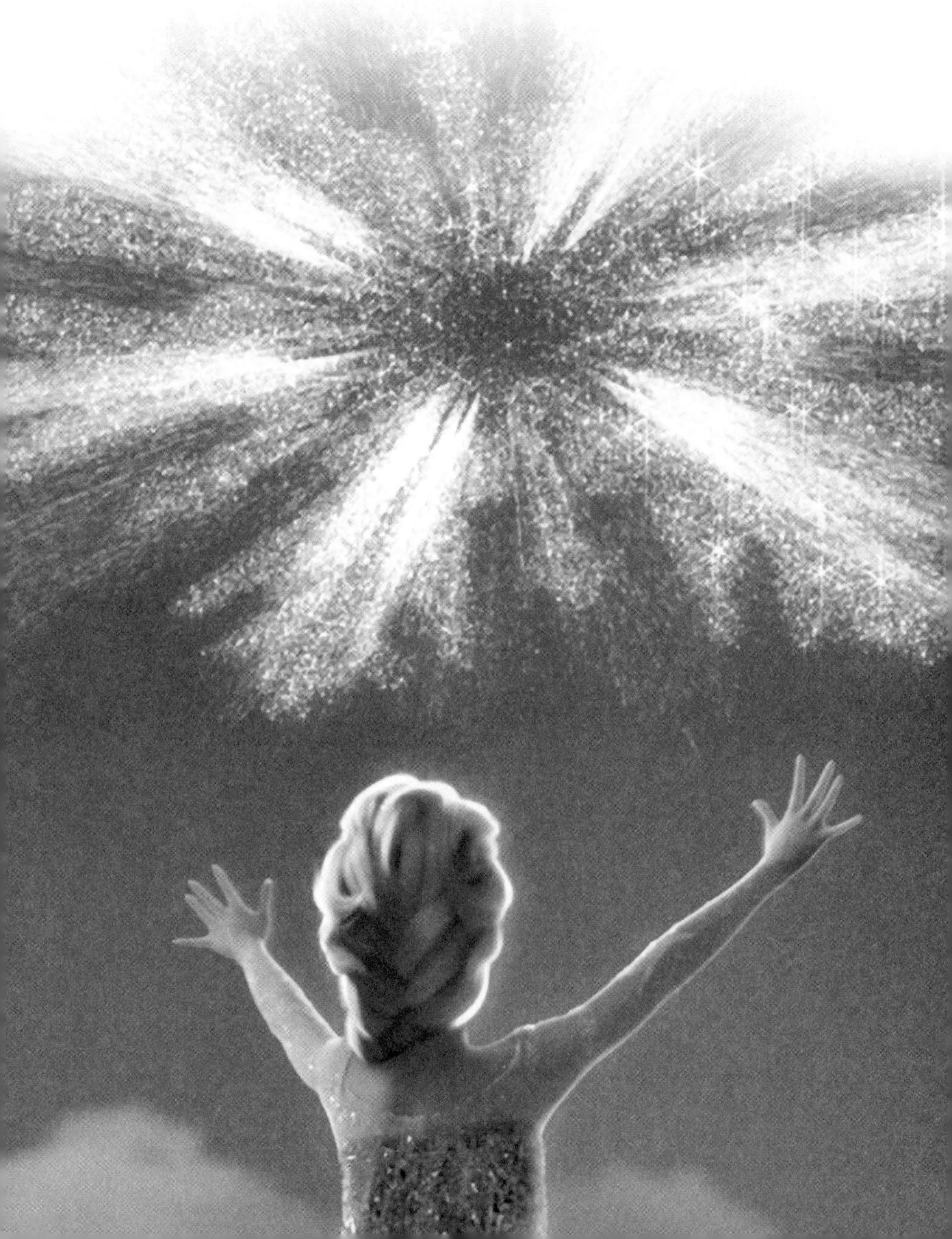

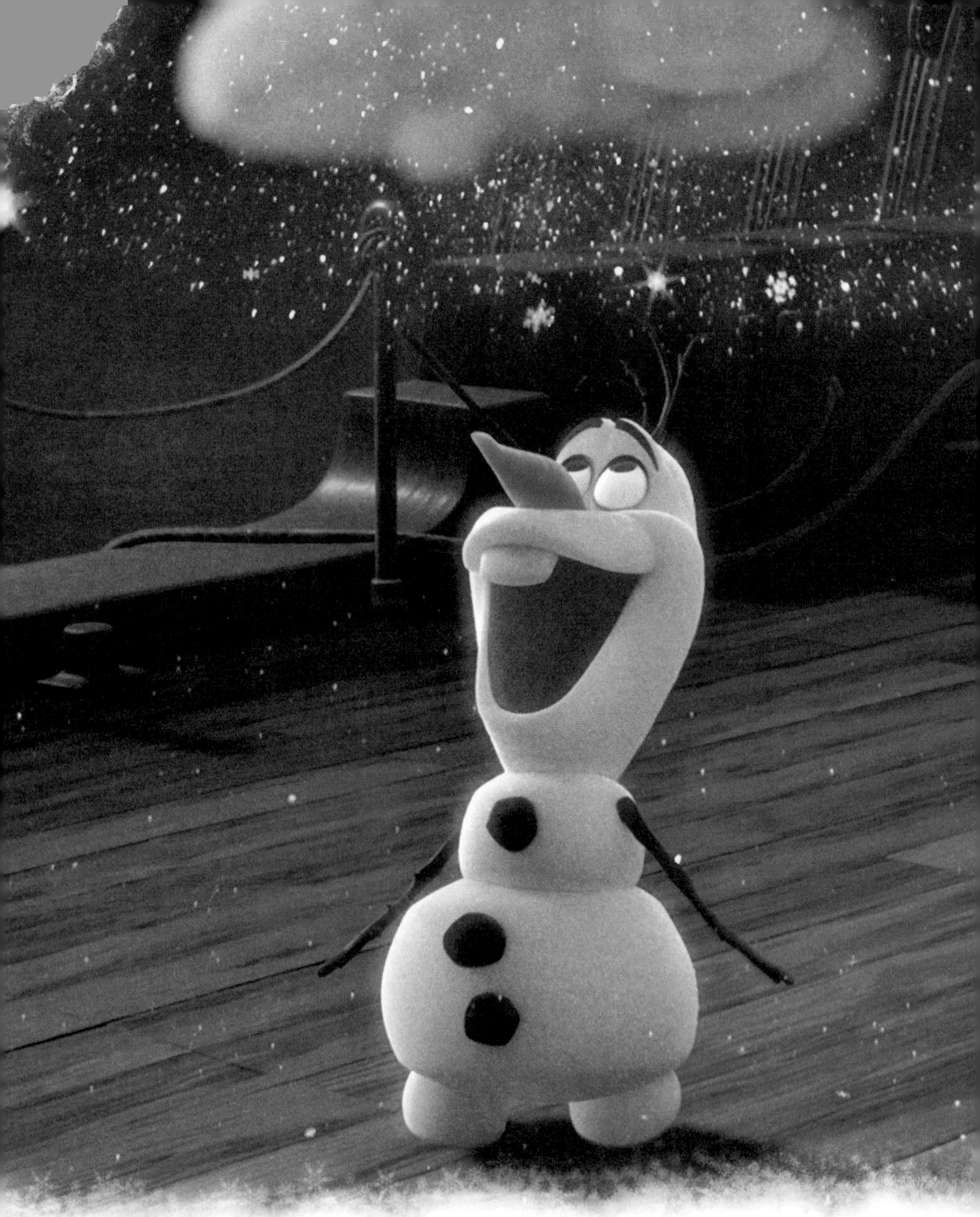

Now Olaf the snowman
will never melt!